Liftoff!

Edited by David Booth

Steck-Vaughn®

 HOUGHTON MIFFLIN HARCOURT

10801 N. Mopac Expressway
Building # 3
Austin, TX 78759
1.800.531.5015

Steck-Vaughn is a trademark of HMH Supplemental Publishers Inc.
registered in the United States of America and/or other jurisdictions.
All inquiries should be mailed to HMH Supplemental Publishers Inc.,
P.O. Box 27010, Austin, TX 78755.

Rubicon
www.rubiconpublishing.com

Associate Publisher: Wendy Cochran
Editorial Assistant: Dawna McKinnon
Creative/Art Director: Jennifer Drew
Senior Designer: Jeanette Debusschere
Cover image–NASA; title page–iStockphoto.com

Printed in Singapore

ISBN: 978-1-77058-454-9
1 2 3 4 5 6 7 8 9 10   2016   21 20 19 18 17 16 15 14 13 12
A B C D E F G

Contents

SPACE

There is no air in space.
But there is a sun.

There is no rain in space.
But there are stars.

There are no dust storms
in space.
But there is dust.

There is lots of space in space.
But is there space for me?

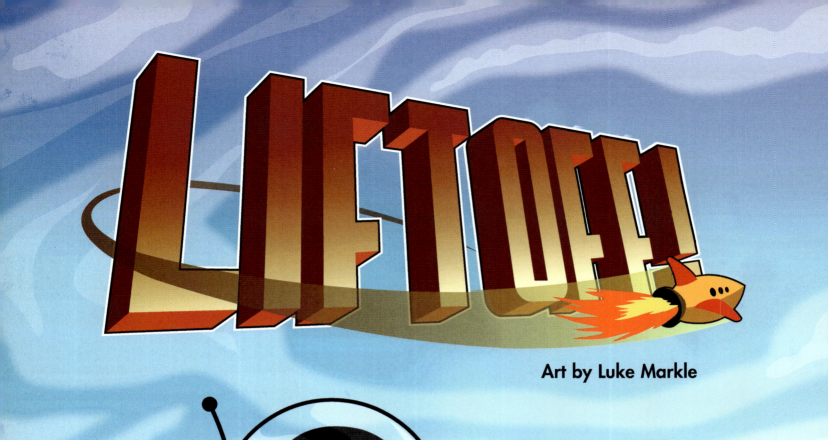

LIFTOFF!

Art by Luke Markle

One is one and two is two.
I'm an astronaut. What are you?

Three is three and four is four.
Listen to my spaceship roar.

Five is five and six is six.
Come onboard, we must be quick!

Seven is seven, eight is eight.
Want to be my teammate?

Nine is nine and ten is ten.
I will start to count again.

One is one and two is two.
I will share my ship with you.

10

Three is three and four is four.
Do not open any door!

Five is five and six is six.
Come and see an astronaut's tricks!

Seven is seven, eight is eight.
Hurry up! We can't be late!

Nine is nine and ten is ten.
When will you see Earth again?

Ten
nine
eight
seven
six
five
four
three
two
one ...

LIFTOFF!

Look at what I see:

The sun

The moon

The Planets

The Stars

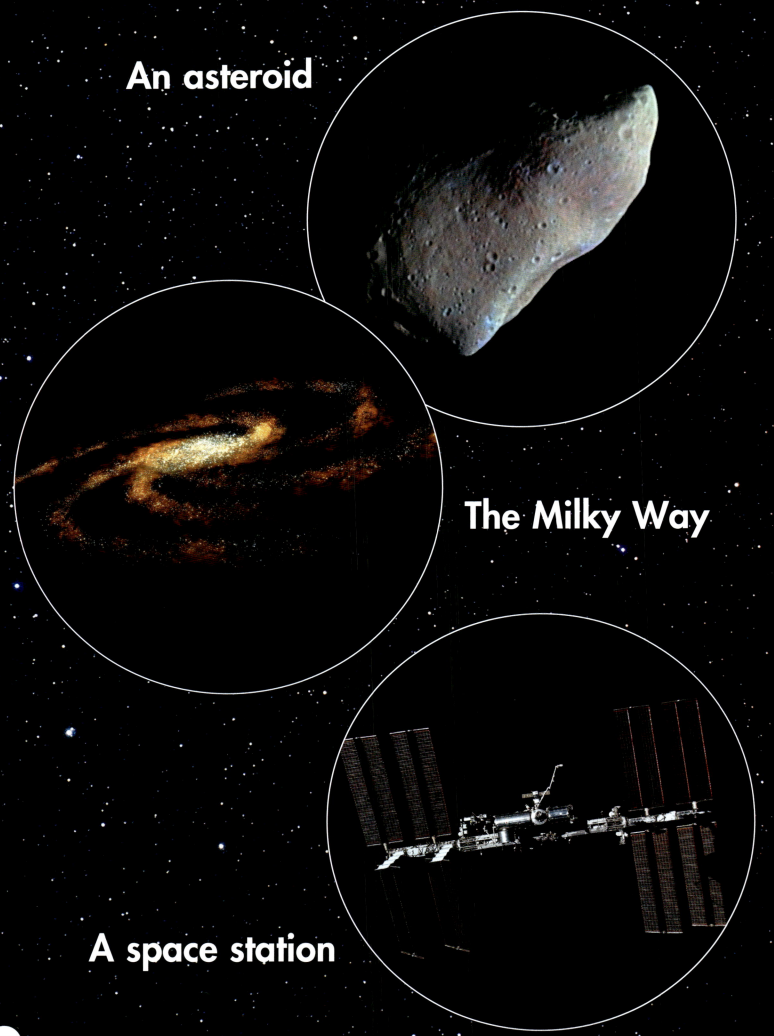

An asteroid

The Milky Way

A space station

A GIANT FLY!

That's what I see
in the GREAT BIG SKY
with your super eye.

But with my eye,
all that I spy
is a tiny, tiny fly.

CREATURES

By Larry Swartz

This strange creature has a face. It has two arms that go around and around and around. What is it?

TiCK! TOCK!

VROOM!
VROOM!

It must be an alien!

Meet Commander Collins

Eileen Collins always loved airplanes. She took flying lessons when she was 19 years old. Later, she became a pilot in the U.S. Air Force.

Eileen Collins became
the first woman
to pilot a space shuttle.

FYI
Eileen Collins has
spent more than
870 hours in space.

Then she became commander
of a space shuttle.
She has won many awards.

Rocket Boy

Art by Martin Wittfooth

Noah put on his pyjamas.
He brushed his teeth.
It was time for bed.

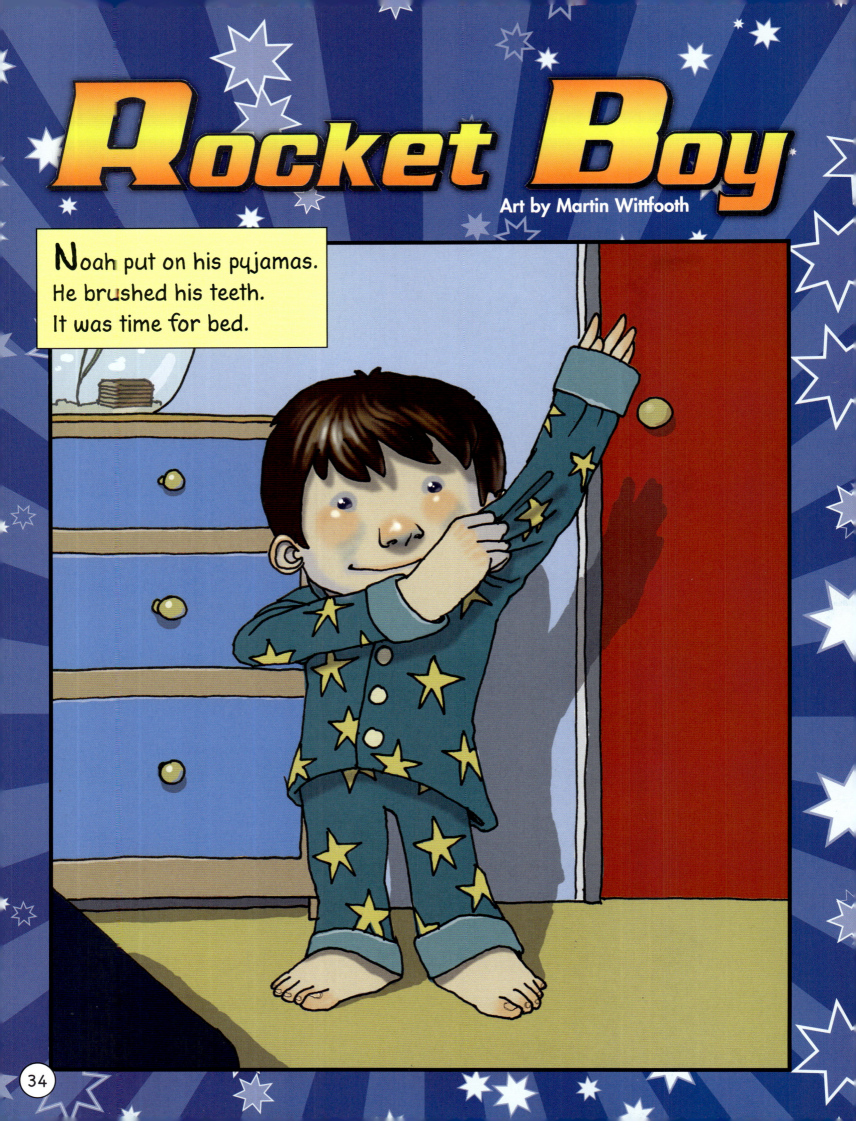

Star light, star bright
First star I see tonight

He read a book with his dad.

His dad kissed him good night.

The room grew dark.

Noah could see the moon through his window.

It's time!

He rolled out of bed
and slipped his rocket pack
over his shoulders.

Shhhhhh!

Noah tiptoed across the room.
He opened his closet door.

He found a small door at the back of the closet.

He opened the small door and went down a tunnel.

At the end of the tunnel was a forest.

He STREAKED past a bird.

Whoops!

He **soared** by a plane.

That was close!

He **ZOOOOOMED** around a space station.

Hello ...

But then, the rocket **sputtered.**

Oh no!

Whhooooaaa!

Phew!

He landed with a soft thud.

He ran up the tunnel and into the closet.

He opened the closet door and jumped into bed.

Just then, his mother came into his room.

44

MOON MIX-UP

On July 20, 1969
men walked on the moon for the first time.

Put the pictures in order to tell the story.

Neil Armstrong, Michael Collins, and Edwin Aldrin
were astronauts on *Apollo 11.*

ALL IMAGES—NASA